THE GHOST
AFFECT

This book is a work of fiction. Names, characters, places, and incidents are the product of the author's imagination or are used fictitiously. Any character that happens to share the same name as an acquaintance of the author, past or present, is purely coincidental and is in no way an actual account involving that person. Any other resemblance to actual events, locales, or persons, living, or dead, is coincidental.

If you purchase this book without a cover you should be aware that this book may have been stolen property and reported as "unsold and destroyed" to the publisher. In such cases neither the author nor the publisher has received any payment for this "stripped book."

Copyright © 2022 The Ghost Affect by Chrissy Good & Michael Good. All rights reserved. Except as permitted under the U.S. Copyright Act of 1976, no part of this publication may be reproduced, distributed, or transmitted in any form or by any means, or stored in a database or retrieval system, without the prior written permission of the publisher.

The Mike Midas Publishing name and logo is a trademark of Beat Murda Music Group, LLC.

For more information on the author please visit his website:
http://readmrgoodgoeshard.com or email
readmrgoodgoeshard@gmail.com

Instagram: @Mrgoodgoeshardtheauthor

Twitter: @readmggh

Printed in the United States of America

GHOST AFFECT

Imagine you're inside of a tunnel or an elevator and you suddenly start to feel woozy and like you're going to faint on the spot. But then this feeling goes away as suddenly as it started. This is considered the ghost affect.

What is the ghost affect you may ask? Do you feel that cold draft on the back of your neck? The hairs are standing up, aren't they? Goosebumps all along your flesh. That is the ghost of a person latching onto you.

This ghost comes from out of nowhere latching onto any unsuspecting person to feed off of their souls. These ghosts have died from unnatural causes and do not possess the ability to move on so they in turn will possess a living breathing person instead. The ghosts will then invade the person's brain so that that person can feel what the ghost felt as it was dying; thus the ghost affect.

It's been said the only way to rid these ghostly possessions is to perform a seance in front of a computer screen. The ghost gets trapped inside the screen and cannot return to the world afterwards unless it has been summoned, so it will walk around its own purgatory until it is ready to pass on.

Click. That's the power button on the computer being turned on. The candles have all been lit. The people are sitting around the table holding hands. The medium begins her ritual. The air around begins to turn cold. They can hear subtle screams all around them like voices that are trapped inside of a portal trying to get out. One woman starts to suddenly convulse claiming she is being stabbed in the back. She falls over off of her chair unable to move.

Another woman is claiming she is in labor but she is not pregnant. She begins to feel the blood rushing out of her vagina but there is nothing there and then she proceeds to pass out. A man is drowning. He starts to regurgitate imaginary water out of his lungs. He soon stops breathing but comes back to life just as suddenly as he started to drown.

More and more people start to "die" and then come back just as quickly as they died. This goes on for a mere five minutes before the medium explodes with a loud voice saying" STOP! WE KNOW YOU ARE HERE WITH US. WE CAN FEEL YOU. WE KNOW YOU ARE IN PAIN AND WISH TO BE RELEASED. COME TO THE LIGHT AND YOU WILL BE RELEASED."

One by one the men and women around the table all begin to sit up in a daze as if confused and no longer aware of their surroundings. The medium produces her globe that is filled with some sort of bright light. And one by one they start to see spirits descend into the globe. Most of the ghosts have moved on.

A few have stayed back. The people sitting around the table can still hear subtle screaming but it's not as loud as before. The medium begins to explain the reasoning behind the computer and what it will allow to happen to all of the ghosts who are left who feel like they still have unfinished business.

As the medium and the others turn towards the computer screen, the ghostly howls become much clearer as if they know what is about to happen and they are afraid. The medium starts her second ritual and chants out to the ghosts to release the people they are holding onto and enter into the computer realm. As her chanting gets louder and louder so do the ghostly screams.

The chanting goes up an octave and they begin to see spirits descending from what looks like the backs of the mens and womens necks as if that's where they were latched onto. The ghosts enter into the computer realm unaware that they are completely trapped.

The medium turns the computer off and all is silent again. "So how does this happen, this ghost affect?" one person asked. "Well," replies the medium, " after a person dies if a spirit feels that it has some unfinished business it will seek out a human to latch itself onto until that human finds out what has happened to the body of the spirit that has died or in our case we trap the soul."

The people, being cured of their affliction, all go home to their families unsuspecting that one such ghost has been released from its prison inside the computer screen and is now searching for another living body to latch onto. The ghost, unable to travel as a spirit freely, instead travels the circuits until it finds another computer screen to escape from.

A detective is walking home one night and enters into his domain to settle in for the night and rest. He flicks on his computer screen and begins to type up his report for the next day. Whir, click. His computer boots up. Suddenly, the air around him turns chilly and he gets goosebumps along his flesh and feels a slight tug at the back of his neck that begins to form a headache. Thinking nothing of it, he gets up from his desk to turn the heat up a notch.

As he is settling back into his desk chair to finish his report, his headache begins to worsen. There is a sharp pain at the back of his neck and he passes out. When he wakes up he looks up signs of strokes and aneurysms feeling that he is still too young to have these feelings but it doesn't hurt to investigate anyway.

He comes across a report about what is called the Ghost Affect. Thinking that anything helps before he goes to a doctor to check himself out, he starts to dig around the missing persons database for anyone who maybe has died from the ailments he is experiencing. He comes across one such man who disappeared about thirty miles from where the detective lives.

The detective takes a drive that way to see if he can find the missing body so he can set the spirit free before he starts to experience more of the symptoms he had experienced in his home. He has a couple more attacks on his way to where the person went missing, so it is taking him longer than normal.

He enters into the little town of the missing person and begins his investigation by asking the people of this town if any of them knew what might have happened to this person. One such man tells him where the person he is looking for lived before she went missing. The man goes to the person's house and looks around for any clues.

There are woods surrounding the area. The man searches the woods hoping to find this body so he can be rid of its spirit and the ailments that come with it. Upon coming up to a boulder near a lake, he sees what looks like a pair of shoes poking from behind the big rock. The man walks over to the boulder and sees the body of an older woman who has fallen out. Her face is distorted and her limbs are laid out at different angles. Another attack is approaching so the man sets his laptop down and turns it on before he is afflicted once again.

He read up on ways to rid this body of its ghostly spirit before he came out this way. It is said that there are certain chants that can be read aloud and it will rid a body of its ghost and the ghost will then move on, so the man begins his ritual. His chanting gets louder and louder like a crescendo and he begins to hear slight howls and screams. "Move towards the light young lady. I know you are wishing to be free. I have found your body and I will give you a beautiful memorial so as to honor your memory."

Suddenly the howls and screams end as suddenly as it began. The man calls for a coroner to come and take the body to the nearest morgue and proceeds to conduct a memorial service as he promised the woman he would do. The service is short and simple but her memory will live on in the little town. The man then heads back to his own house in his own city and sits back at his computer to finish his paperwork from the night before. If you listen closely you can still hear slight howls coming from his computer but the man is so wrapped up in his work that he doesn't have the slightest clue he might again be the next victim of another ghost attack.

JUPITERS COLLISION: THE FOUND JOURNAL

We've set out to find other survivors. We know there are other survivors but the radios are all static now. When the nuclear bombs were detonated a few of us hid underground to wait it out. To wait until the shaking from the explosions had stopped. To wait for the air to clear up a bit. We are running low on supplies, so we must go in search of more. Those of us who have made it through this seemingly endless nightmare are trying not to go as insane as those who couldn't handle knowing their world may not be as it was before.

I should start at the beginning. The year is 2045. One day the world was safe and still intact; by the end of the next day those of us able to get away from the horrors we were witnessing (bombs exploding; earthquakes of mega proportions; the oceans spilling over; the lights) went underground. We were able to contact a few survivors but then, nothing. Static. There was one survivor in particular. A father of two children; a husband. He told us about these particular lights in the sky he had seen. Oceanic waves of lights. Like the oceans and the sky had switched places. He had an odd note to his voice, like he was hypnotized. He informed us of his coordinations and told us if we found his family to reassure him that he was safe. That was nearly fifteen years ago. So we left our safe haven to go in search of supplies and other possible survivors.

When we had resurfaced to the top, we saw these lights. It was like the whole sky was gone. There was just...an ocean of beautifully colored lights. They seemed to have been coming from north of where we were bunkered. My partners and I agreed that that must be the place the man we had spoken to fifteen years ago must be. Assuming he was still alive. Still, we were convinced we needed to check it out. There had to be other survivors. We survived, right?

We had walked several miles before we first saw the tunnel. The earth had changed so much in all the years we were down under.

The trees became one with the leaves. The leaves were no longer forests of green; now there were bright greens mixed in with bluish green colors. The grass had these kinds of tusks growing up with reddish hues. Plastic was the word that came to mind, and yet they were as real as you and me. Animals seemed to have become extinct. It felt like we were in some kind of alternate reality. Or on an alien planet. And by the time we had reached the tunnel half of us were pale and starving from lack of wanting to eat or sleep.

We found a journal on the way to the tunnels. Seems it had been the surviving father's daughter's journal. We confirmed that this must be the place where he had radioed us from, so we took a look around to see if we could locate him. As my partners were assessing the place, I sat down near a tree to read the journal. The daughter stated that her father had been gone for several weeks before they set out to search for him. She had described in her writings of witnessing her mother and brother being overcome with a hypnosis-like demeanor such as my partners and I had felt. She also stated that her brother and mother hadn't eaten or slept in several days due to lack of desire of needing to.

She then goes on to tell of the pods. Pods that her father says they were to step into and then allow gases to overtake the senses to put a body into a deep sleep. That was the end of her journal. Too late, I remembered my partners; because halfway through the partaking of the pod system, the girl described aliens from another planet, the planet of Jupiter and how these ethereal, almost iridescent creatures were here to protect our species and planet from being destroyed by other aliens sent here from the planet Mars.

I ran into the tunnels as fast as I could, trying to warn the others of what I had just ascertained through the girl's journal writings. I couldn't find my partners anywhere. I did, however, encounter one of these aliens. Its backside was turned towards me. It was holding a gold heart shaped locket in its hand. This locket was another object the girl described in her journal; a piece of jewelry given to her by her father in case he never returned. I stood as still as I possibly could, hoping to study this alien; this paragon. It was a stunning sight to behold! Even more stunning than the oceanic waves of light above us! These aliens were more than just mere entities; they were angelic creatures sent here to protect us!

*

When the alien had departed from the area of the pods I decided it was time to take a look around, just to be safe, before I tried to make contact with them; after all my partners were still AWOL. As I was walking towards the pods I detected an obsessive odor coming from them. I took a peek inside one of the pods and found a young girl, no more than the age of twelve. She must be the girl from the journal. She appeared to be asleep but I believed her to be dead. Her pallored face was ashen and I was noticing some discoloration upon her skin. There were others who were starting to decay in their pods as well. A man, the father I presumed; a boy, the brother; and a woman, the mother this girl spoke of in her journal entries. This must be the family the father had told my partners and I about, which I took to mean that these creatures were not sent here to protect us, they were sent here to destroy us.

I ran as quickly as I could towards the exit of the tunnels, making as little noise as possible so as not to alarm the aliens in case one or more of them were nearby. As I was nearing the exit, I heard a noise behind me. The alien holding the locket had noticed me attempting to depart its domain. I keep a mirror in my pack for emergencies such as this; something to deflect light into a creature's eyes if ever I needed to escape certain death. I held the mirror up to the lights coming up out of the tunnels, hoping the reflection would divert its attention, not knowing whether or not it even had eyes to stun. The sound it made coming out of a hole in its face was akin to a fire alarm. It was calling on others! Quickly, I escaped out of the tunnel and hid behind these plastic like trees. I could see the alien following me as well as others coming up out of the tunnels.

I searched for a well rounded tree to hide behind. Once I was there I crouched down and was still, waiting on the aliens to grow bored of trying to find me. Instead, I could see long snouts coming out of their faces, similar to an anteater's snout. They began to sniff the grounds and claw at the earth. I held my breath in anticipation sure they would find me. Alas, their explorations were unsuccessful and I was able to escape without fear of being traced.

I ran through the forests as fast as I could, not even attempting to look back to be sure I wasn't being followed. As soon as I felt I could stop, I slowed down and took a rest so as to clear my head. The girl wrote about another army of aliens from the planet of Mars. I was sure I would run into them if I kept heading away from Jupiters aliens, so I had to ponder my next move. If I backtracked from whence I came I could make it back to my bunker and I would be safe, but without the necessary supplies I needed to survive even a few nights. The only chance I had of surviving the end of the world was to keep going as far as I could while still being alert for more than just mere animals now.

*

My journey towards the east has been long and hard but so far I have not run into anything remotely alien-like. I killed a few deer (if it was a nuclear blast surely the animals would be as dead from radiation poisoning as humans) and a few rabbits. I found a stream and started walking along the edge of it; I caught a few fish to eat out of the river the stream led to and filled all of my canisters with fresh water. I have not found signs of a different species from another planet, but my journey is far from over. There must be other humans alive. I can't be the only one.

I decided that I needed to stop and rest for the night so I set up a tent and a fire and I made an alarm system with sticks of wood to protect myself. I would continue my search for more people and resources in the morning. As I was laying down to sleep I heard a rustling in the woods. It was such a small sound I figured it must be an animal but I kept my ears alert nonetheless.

A few hours of sleep later and I heard another rustling noise. I popped my head up to investigate the noise. As I was climbing out of my tent I noticed some sort of a footprint not human near it. Cautiously, I began to examine my little area where I was squatting. There were more footprints. I decided to pack up and move on to another location. As I was climbing out of my tent I noticed some sort of a footprint not human near it. Cautiously, I began to examine my little area where I was squatting. There were more footprints. I decided to pack up and move on to another location. As I was getting ready to start walking again, there were more noises behind me. I began to run as quickly and as stealthily as I could hoping to outrun whomever or whatever was possibly chasing me.

I had reached the end of the path. I decided to stop and rest for a minute to clear my head and assess my situation. Suddenly I could feel my hands being bent behind my back. It seems something or someone had found me. I fought them off and turned around to find out what had attacked me. I could only ascertain that these aliens attacking me must be the aliens from Mars! They were tall and had stubby faces and big black round eyes. They were talking to me in a language unlike any I had heard before. They're legs were so long I couldn't outrun them and they captured me and knocked me unconscious.

Chrissy Good

I woke up in some kind of a tube. I had a headache and my side was hurting like something had been stabbed into me. I looked down and saw smaller tubes coming out of my side. I tried to raise my head but my neck and my arms were restrained. An alien came back and started adjusting the tubes and my blood started draining out. They also had given me some kind of substance that disintegrated my insides and they started flowing through another tube. I could see my life flashing before my eyes. I could feel unconsciousness creeping up again. The last thought in my head was that I hoped there are other survivors and that they are able to get away.

WHEN THREE WORLDS COLLIDED- THE JOURNAL ENTRIES OF A JANE DOE

Journal Entry Number One:

We've been in this bunker for two days now. I'm not sure what's going on above us yet. The people say it's radiation ash poisoning from all of the nuclear bombs that were unintentionally detonated in the middle of the night. The sirens filled our ears and we ran underground. There's light down here. And food. We have an old citizens band radio to speak to other survivors. We have been able to contact a few others like ourselves. Father will go up top in a few days to check it out.

Journal Entry Number Two:

Father had this bunker built before my brother and I were born to prepare for a situation such as this. People he knew and trusted called him crazy. These same people tried to join us down here but we only have enough room and oxygen for my brother, me, Mother and Father. Father was saddened by the fact that we couldn't help the others. We can still hear bombs going off on the surface.

We are all safe and as content as we can be. For now.

Journal Entry Number Three:

The booms and shaking have finally stopped. Father is preparing to exit the bunker in the next few days. Or nights. It all just blends together anymore. The tensions down here have been high lately. Too much time spent together I guess. We are all worried and fearful. What, if anything, has happened to our world? We think an earthquake bigger than what is normal has occurred. We are beginning to see cracks in our walls that have been built into the ground. Our bunker has three rooms. A living room and kitchen combination area; a bedroom with two beds for my brother and me, and a bed for Mother and Father; and a bathroom that has running water. Father designed a piping system that runs from under our house to the bunker. Father was an architect before the bombs started going off.

Journal Entry Number Four:

Father has been gone for several days now. Or it could be just mere hours, we are not so sure of much of anything anymore. We just know that he has not returned as of yet. My brother wants to go up top to look for him. Mother says to wait for Fathers return. "He will be back!", she tells him. My brother fears something has happened to Father. I fear we are all going stir crazy…

Journal Entry Number Five:

It has been several weeks now since my father exited our bunker. My mother and my brother are preparing us to go in search of him. We have tried to contact others, but to no avail. The cb radio is dying. And thewatersupply will soon run out. We have oxygen tanks we will take with us when we exit, but we only have a few days of use with those. Father gave me a heart shaped locket with a picture of us all inside of it in case he never returned or we got separated from each other, so I will never forget my family. I will always wear it around my neck.

Journal Entry Number Six:

We are preparing to exit the bunker today. Our oxygen masks are on our faces and the oxygen tanks on our backs. We have packed enough food and water to last for several days. It will be sad to leave this new home we have built for ourselves but we are all worried something has happened to Father so we must go off in search of him.

Journal Entry Number Seven:

It has been a long day. We are all settling down to rest and sleep for the night. No sign of Father as of yet. We walked about twenty miles north of our bunker. Mother says tomorrow we will head east. The trees are bare of their leaves. The ground is full of ash and soot. The air, I fear, will still be unbreathable for many days to come.

There is a beautiful light in the sky that was never there until now, though. As soon as we find Father we intend to investigate.

Journal Entry Number Eight:

We are soon to be heading east in search of Father some more. The lights in the sky seem to be getting brighter. And stronger. They are beginning to resemble oceanic waves of light...beautiful colors...

Journal Entry Number Nine:

We have settled in for the night. It is night, we think. The waves of light seem to have blocked out the sun, and yet the stars still peak through every now and then. Still no sign of Father. We have travelled as far as fifteen miles today. Mother says that we need a little more time to rest tonight. Tomorrow we start going south. The lights are stronger towards the south.

Journal Entry Number Ten:

We've started walking south today. The trees this way have more color to them, but brighter than they were before the bombs went off. And different colors than mere trees on earth had. Blueish green colors. The leaves kind of blend in with the trees as well but still have a distinct shape to them. And there is grass yet there is no grass. There are patches in the earth with little tusks of grass growing up with a reddish sort of hue. It is kind of beautiful. The waves of lights in the sky are getting more prominent. Like the earth turned upside down and the ocean is the sky and the sky's the ocean without the water. Mother keeps looking up, more mesmerized by these lights each time. My brother has gone quiet. That is unusual for him. I am worried these lights are affecting us in negative ways.

Journal Entry Number Eleven:

Mother says we have to keep walking south. I think she is hypnotized by the lights. My brother has a dazed look on his face. He hasn't spoken a word in almost a day. We settled in for the night last night. Still no sign of Father.

I keep telling her maybe we should head back to the bunker. I'm worried we are running low on oxygen. Our food and water sources are almost depleted. Mother and my brother don't seem to want to eat; they barely sleep. We just keep walking south. The waves of light are getting stronger. I fear for them but I don't say anything. We just keep walking...

Journal Entry Number Twelve:

It is day number six of our trek now. We are still walking south. Mother claims if we stop we will never find Father. She thinks he is where the lights end. We haven't stopped to sleep or eat in two days. Her and my brother don't even act like themselves anymore. Their eyes are glazed over and their faces are pale, but she insists we keep going. The lights are even more beautiful. Almost ethereal. And the waves are not of this world. We are beginning to slowly start to see where the lights began. It is quite beautiful!

Journal Entry Number Thirteen:

We have come upon an opening where the waves of light flow out of. Mother has a new nervous energy about her, none like I have ever seen before. We are going to investigate what is under the ground where the lights flow. It is some kind of a tunnel. We can see Father at the end of this tunnel. He is here! We have found him at last! Oh, I am so happy. We can finally rest. He says he has something to show us. Some new friends to meet. He has the same glazed over look in his eyes as well. These friends though, they are not ordinary. They don't look like us. They seem more iridescent. We are leaving this underground tunnel. The beings protecting us have a safer place for us to go. A place they say is like no place we have ever witnessed before with our own eyes but we have to drift into a deep sleep. We are being led to some pods. My body is beginning to feel as if I am no longer a part of it. I wonder if this is how my brother, Mother and Father felt. There is some kind of gas pouring into my pod. I am feeling very sleepy. My eyelids are getting very heavy. This will be my last entry into my journal for a while. I wonder what it will be like when we reach our destination? Father tells me I need to rest for our long journey ahead. A bad feeling makes my stomach flutter with anticipation. I am trying not to worry, to just be calm and allow the gas to overtake my senses. If anyone ever finds this journal please search for us. I have to sleep now.

Father says they are safe. He says they are here to take care of us. That Mars and Jupiter collided with Earth and that the beings from Mars tried to kill us earthlings so these iridescent beings from Jupiter are here to protect what is left of our world. That when we heard bombs detonating it was really our three worlds colliding; we were never in danger of radiation poisoning.

Journal Entry Number Fourteen:

I miss my old life. I miss my home. Mother and Father don't seem like themselves anymore. My brother is paler than usual. He still has a glazed look in his eyes. I still keep the locket Father gave me around my neck. The unearthly beings want to take us out of this tunnel. Mother and Father beg me to follow them. I am scared but I will go. I should eat but I don't feel hungry anymore. Father is excited to be leaving this tunnel soon. He tells me all will be well. I am not so sure it will be.

Journal Entry Number Fifteen:

We are leaving this underground tunnel. The beings protecting us have a safer place for us to go. A place they say is like no place we have ever witnessed before with our own eyes but we have to drift into a deep sleep. We are being led to some pods. My body is beginning to feel as if I am no longer a part of it. I wonder if this is how my brother, Mother and Father felt. There is some kind of gas pouring into my pod. I am feeling very sleepy. My eyelids are getting very heavy. This will be my last entry into my journal for a while. I wonder what it will be like when we reach our destination? Father tells me I need to rest for our long journey ahead. A bad feeling makes my stomach flutter with anticipation. I am trying not to worry, to just be calm and allow the gas to overtake my senses. If anyone ever finds this journal please search for us. I have to sleep now.

THE WAR OF THE WORLDS: THE LAST HUMANS LEFT

In the year 2031 there was a collision between Jupiter, Mars and Earth. Jupiter and Mars joined Earth to form one planet. This collision detonated nuclear bombs all over the world. Earthquakes of mega proportions formed. Aliens roamed the Earth. Destruction at its best. Those who could hide underground did; those who couldn't, encountered either nuclear radiation or risked coming face to face with aliens who were intent on taking over Earth.

Jupiters aliens formed an underground tunnel full of pods where they took humans to put them to "sleep", claiming they were trying to help these people escape Mars' aliens. One particular survivor was a man, one of the first humans to be grounded to the pods, who convinced his family that all was well and not to fear what was being done to them. A little girl wrote about this in her journal telling a story of how her father had given her a heart shaped locket filled with a picture of the family in case they were ever to be separated from each other.

Mars' aliens formed tubes that held humans to rid them of their insides and blood as the aliens experimented on them. The Earth began to transform into a planet not like any seen before by human eyes. The trees and leaves were as one with bright green and bluish colors; the grass had tusks growing out of the ground with a red hue; and the sky was filled with beautifully colored, almost surreal lights covering the sunlight and the stars.

These aliens were at war with one another to see who could take over the planet. The people left on earth who had not died from the destruction of the planet or who had not ran into the aliens themselves were nevertheless still bystanders amidst this war. They built underground bunkers to keep themselves safe and only came out to scavenge for supplies when necessary, or to search for other survivors. Only a few hundred thousand people were left on Earth.

The war lasted for many years. There were bodies of humans as well as aliens strewn in any which direction. The lights in the sky caused a hypnosis-like effect on anyone who looked at them, luring them to the underground tunnels where they were captured and put to sleep. People began to suspect the lights of having this effect, so the ones who noticed the effects of others started wearing sunglasses to block out the rays in terms of keeping them from losing their own thought processes.

There began to form a resistance among the humans. They were to fight back with any means necessary to keep the aliens who held them captive from completely taking over Earth, albeit the other two planets were as of now one planet amongst the three. The people of the planet set up their own weapons of mass destruction formed out of pipe bombs and explosives. They set up land mines that, when stepped on, would blow up any aliens coming within range of their bunkers.

A city was created underground that spanned across the globes. With three planets, there was more space to roam. Trade began to resume. Individual and family housings were built into the cave walls. Occasionally loud booms were heard topside, in hopes that it was an alien who was destroyed and not another human, for too many had been lost fighting to survive this ongoing war. New businesses were built. Gardens were designed to grow vegetables and edible plants. Cattle, chickens and other animals used for meat adapted to the underground to be killed and eaten.

Until one day some of the people grew weary of having to stay underground for days on end. The resistance decided it was time to fight back, so they began to salvage weapons left over from demolished aliens. They began to establish weapons that would be grand enough to destroy the last of the aliens who hadn't been killed off by each other. Weapons that were greater than any nuclear arsenal ever designed.

The people who formed this resistance set out to hunt the aliens and destroy them. They hunted from one end of the new planet to the other until all were captured or taken out. As the last of the aliens were destroyed, the resistance returned home triumphant over their victory. It took many years and many people died fighting, but the war of the ages was finally over.

One by one the people of the new planet began to venture towards the topside. The animals and plants were uprooted from underground to adapt to the new planet. Cities and houses were rebuilt. The people became one nation set out to rebuild their lives. Sunglasses were a permanent attachment to their faces, but as long as they wore them they could contain their own thoughts. The lands would be made whole again. The Earth would replenish itself. All who were left would be well and life would go on as it should and the resistance were now prepared for another attack should it ever happen again.

A CASE OF THE BLUES

There's a city that's not on any map known to man. The people in this city have come down with a case of the blues. It was a once happy city. The people were always smiling and joking and laughing. Then one day a woman who was flying across the continents came upon this unknown city and landed her plane there.

She was welcomed with open arms by all. They fed her and befriended her and made her feel she was always welcome no matter what so long as she kept their little city a secret. She promised them she would always return for a visit but would bring no one with her and no one would know of this place but her. Then she sets off to finish her flight around the world.

A Case Of The Blues

The people of this city go about their lives smiling and laughing and living the way they want to live with no one interrupting their joyous lives. One day, one of the women of this city starts to frown for some unknown reason. She claims she doesn't know why, she just doesn't feel like smiling anymore. Then her skin begins to turn blue.

They quarantine her to the outskirts of the city checking up on her from time to time thinking that it is some kind of a disease that can be spread and hoping it doesn't spread throughout the city to the rest of the happy folk. After about a week she still has a blue pallor but her smile returns so they think nothing of it and allow her to return to her everyday mundane tasks of being happy and smiling and always laughing.

A few weeks later, another woman begins to frown. Thinking that she has caught the "bug" she removes herself from the others and quarantines in the same spot the other woman quarantined herself. She notices a few days later that her arms have turned blue. She is afraid that if she returns to the city before she starts to feel better that she will infect the others so she stays quarantined for longer than recommended.

The first woman to be infected with the blues, a few weeks later, still smiling and happy, starts to feel her frown coming back. Her arms are still blue but her face and neck begin to turn the same color. She is scared and feeling reckless, so she sets out to quarantine herself with the other woman. They both go over what might have caused this ailment, neither of them having a clue where to begin. Nothing like this has ever been an issue in all of the years they have occupied this city.

As the weeks pass, one by one the women of the city begin to lose their laughs and giggles and frowns begin to replace their smiles. Not knowing what to do, they all abandon their men and children to quarantine themselves so they don't spread the infection. Their skin starts to turn blue starting on their arms and soon ends up being all over them.

So now there is a spot on the outskirts of this little city that has never known of anything but happiness and laughter filled with blue women who have constant frowns upon their faces. The men of the city start to investigate what has caused these ailments to inflict their women and go about searching all over their city in hopes of finding a cure.

The scientists that occupy this city take samples of the land and observe the samples under a microscope coming up with nothing that will give them clues to how this ailment came about, so they inquire on the philosophers of the city to question how this may have happened. The philosophers question the women on their whereabouts and their tasks they have performed for many decades still coming up short.

The women all sit around in a circle pondering themselves on what could have caused this ailment. One woman remembers the lady that flew to their city and wonders if maybe she had anything to do with what has caused their sudden frowns and blue colored skin, so they tell the men to go in search of this lady and find her and bring her back to their city.

The men start their quest on finding the lady. They search the skies in their planes. They search the seas in their boats to no avail. They return to the city disappointed and frustrated wishing they could be with their women smiling and happy and laughing.

One day, as the women are huddling around a fire cooking dinner for each other, they see a plane heading towards them. It seems the lady has returned at last. They begin to question her as to why they have been afflicted with this disease of not being able to hold a smile or a laugh anymore and as to why it has turned their skin so blue. The lady in turn answers the questions by saying, " but my dears. You were too happy all the time. Who wants to be happy every minute of every day? Where's the fun in that? Where's the fun in not controlling your men and the daily tasks they take on each day? Someone had to wipe the fucking smirks off of your faces." And she produces an evil laugh.

The women contact their men and inform them of what has been told after they have coerced the lady into staying with them for the night. The men begin to build a massive bonfire filling it with as many sticks and would as they could find, then they produce a skewer big enough to hold several fully grown men. The men and women of the city all sit together and chat with the lady tricking her into thinking that she is always welcome to their city.

As they settle in for the night and the lady who goes by the name of Emily starts to snore, the men spray a chemical up her nose to ensure that she stays asleep and then they tie her up to the skewer and light the bonfire. She awakens to the smell of smoke and pain in her legs and begins to scream out, " What are you doing? Are you trying to kill me and then eat me?" " Yes," the women reply. " That is exactly what we are doing. You came into our homes and destroyed what he has built ourselves for many decades. You are evil and we are going to cleanse ourselves and our city of your evilness."

As the fire rages on and the screams get louder, the women of the city begin to smile and laugh again and the color of their skin is no longer blue. They all enjoy a nice sit down dinner together and feed the bones and scraps to the animals. The next day they all wake up and resume their lives as it was before the lady named Emily brought her evil ways to the city, laughing and smiling with not one tear or frown upon their faces. There are now posts outside of the city. They are prepared in case this should ever happen again.

TEN SECONDS

Maury had heard about the ten second rule. Ten seconds to cross the bridge before it starts to shake and twist and you are thrown off of it into the abyss by monsters from another planet. Ten seconds of your life flashing before your eyes. If you make it to the end of the bridge you live.

The bridge is called The Thrill of Your Life. It's a thrill ride at an amusement park; only the aliens are real life paid actors. Everyone from across the world comes to walk this bridge, but you only have ten seconds to cross or…well, you die.

Maury had never gone on this thrill ride before. He had heard of survivors but not that many. The rest fell into the abyss. Considering that he was going on seventy years of age and hadn't done much with his life, he thought what the hell. I don't have anything else to live for I may as well.

So Maury seeks out The Thrill Of Your Life at the amusement park and walks up to it. He can barely make out the alien creatures at the end of the bridge. It's about a mile long and about six feet across with no cables to hold onto to help walk across it, just open space. Below is more open space. A dark hole. This is said to be the most thrilling ride in all of the world and Maury is determined to discover that truth out for himself.

Maury stands at the beginning of the bridge holding out to begin walking across it. He steps one foot onto the bridge and can feel its rickety movements. As Maury starts to cross, his footing becomes more and more unstable so he slows down remembering he only has ten seconds to cross a one mile bridge or risk facing his death into a dark abyss.

Maury speeds up his footing to finish his two mile trek across a bridge that has no cables to hold onto and that is only six feet wide; that also has monsters at the end to tip this bridge over once the ten seconds are up. He is halfway there when he begins to feel the bridge wobbling. "Woah," he exclaims. "That's not supposed to happen yet. I'm only six seconds in." Maury speeds up as quickly as he can without tipping the bridge over himself.

He is a quarter of the way there by now with only three seconds left and the bridge starts to sway back and forth even more. There's nothing to hold onto and Maury can feel himself start to fall off of the edge. He scoots down onto his butt and dangles off of the side of the bridge and crosses his hands one over the other. He tells himself not to look down but can't help it. He does it anyway.

Nothing. There is nothing below him. Just a dark and empty hole. No echoes, no lights, just emptiness. The bridge sways back and forth harder and harder; faster and faster. Maury moves his hands as quickly as they can go fearing that he's not going to make it. He can hear cackles from the end as if the aliens beings are making fun of him. "Fuck you, you dirty rotten whores. I'll not let you take me alive. You'll have to kill me yourself before I end up in that black hole."

The laughter gets worse, yet so do the sways. Almost there, he thinks with one second left. His hand is by the last footing of the bridge and he feels the bridge finally tip over onto its back. He can see the black hole coming up at him so he closes his eyes prepared for nothingness still holding onto the bridge with everything he has.

Maury starts to feel the bridges' swaying slow down, surprised he is still holding on. He can hear the laughter coming from up top. He stays as silent as possible so as not to let them in on the fact that he made it through this hell. As soon as he hears footsteps descend, he climbs back up and proceeds to finish his course. He nears the end and steps over the edge of the bridge. He has made it through the ten seconds of hell!

Maury calmly walks away from the bridge called The Thrill of Your Life alive and well going through the worst yet most exciting evening of his life. Unbeknownst to him, he has to finish his quest through a maze. Feeling as if he is going in circles he retraces his steps so as not to make the same mistakes and redirects his path.

Finally coming upon an opening, Maury steps through it and looks around. He feels as if he has been on this ride for hours but when he looks at his clock he has only been walking for thirty minutes. Thirty minutes of his life wasted by almost dying. Thirty minutes of his life in a daze; Hell in a maze.

He finishes his trek and comes out to the beginning of the park in a haze. No one seems to notice he was even gone. Of course he is seventy with no real family to look after him and no real life to have lived but he still did it.

He walks to the entrance to the park and there stands the two aliens with confused looks on their faces. "Thought you'd killed me didn't you?" Maury remarks. " Well, take a good long look at who I am. I'm a survivor. I've survived your ten seconds of Hell. Fuck you and the horseship your mama rode in on". And Maury heads out the entrance with his shoulders slumped and limping. He turns back one last time to stare at the still confused aliens and throws both of his middle fingers up in the air and leaves the amusement park still alive, a feat not many before him have accomplished.

HAIR OF THE DOG

The man walked up to his homemade moonshine still and poured himself a drink. Little does he know this will be the last drink of his life. A parasite has been growing inside of it.

This parasite landed on the Earth about three hundred years ago and has been buried underground ever since. It made a home inside of the ground awaiting orders from its master letting it know when the right time to come out and take over the planet would be.

The parasite comes up out of the ground on a bright and sunny day searching for a host to infect so that it may walk among the humans and animals that roam this planet. As it was squirming around on its belly like a worm it came upon a moonshine still out in the middle of the woods. It approaches the still and proceeds to enter into the corn spun liquor.

The man drinks his last drop of moonshine on this day. He goes back into his house and settles in with his glass to watch some television before passing out for the night. In his drunken stupor, he feels a slight tickle in his nose, goes to sneeze and blood gushes out instead.

He goes to the bathroom to put some tissue on his nose and tilts his head back. His mama always told him that was the way to stop the bleeding. Once he finds out the bleeding has stopped, he settles back into his chair to finish his drink and his movie.

The parasite that has entered his body has moved into his brain by then. The parasite finds his motor functions and begins to operate them by hooking tiny suction cups into his frontal lobe. This causes the man to become impaired. Thinking that he made the moonshine a little too strong, the man giggles but thinks nothing of it.

The parasite cautiously begins to control the man with his suction cups causing him to slap himself in the face. The man is jarred awake by the sudden slap to the face.

A bit dazed, he looks around at his surroundings being sure that he is still in his home in his chair in front of his television. 'The moonshiners must really be strong this time,' he thinks. 'Its causing me to have dreams of slapping myself'. He chuckles at that and proceeds to fall back asleep.

The parasite, upon ensuring the man is indeed in a deep enough sleep, begins to take over the frontal lobe of the man's brain controlling his thoughts along with his motor functions. He makes the man wake up out of his deep slumber and put some coffee on so he can sober up a bit. Then, when he is done drinking his coffee, the parasite makes the man get dressed and put his shoes on as if he were going to a job. The man still thinks he is asleep but dreaming so he thinks nothing of his movements.

The parasite coerces the man to start walking towards his truck so that he can drive into the nearest town. The man begins to drive along the back roads towards a convenience store set off to the side. They pull into the parking lot of the store. The parasite has the man climb out of his truck and walk towards the front of the store. They go inside the building and look around as if trying to find items to buy. The man picks up a beer and takes it to the counter.

"A dollar thirty-five," says the clerk. The parasite orders the man to walk around the counter and begins to choke the clerk out. He proceeds to kill the clerk. Once the job has been finished the parasite walks back out to the truck and they drive away to another destination.

They find a pawn shop that houses weapons of all kinds. The parasite, knowing that he can do little to nothing with his size, orders the man to purchase two rifles; an AK-47; a Bowie knife; and a couple of smaller hunting knives along with a machete and an axe. They drive farther into town hunting for more victims.

Each stop they make is another kill. Axes to the heads, rifle holes in bodies, stab wounds impaling others. The town soon becomes a bloodbath of gore. Searching the town for any survivors, the parasite again orders the man to move on to the next town. The parasite is in search of a mate to populate the Earth with so that total invasion will go forward as planned.

The people of the next town are slaughtered and slewn in their houses and in their shops. All but one victim is dead.

Hair Of The Dog

The man knocks her out and ties her up as he is ordered to do so and carries her to his truck. They head back to the man's house. The parasite begins to replicate itself so that it may take over the mind of the woman whom it has kidnapped. The replicate parasite enters into the woman's brain and attaches itself into her frontal lobe. They are both ordered back to the man's truck in search of new victims of Earth to dispose of.

They drive all along the country murdering and slaughtering those that are helpless in fighting back and reproducing with those that refuse to stay dead. The parasites have increased from one to many all across the Earth. Few humans are left that have not been invaded. The deed has been done. The parasite that has started this mission leaves the man's body to conquer another planet.

Little did the man know that day that a few years later he would take his last breath helping aliens take over the Earth in his drunken stupor. He called his moonshine Hair Of The Dog and had plans to sell it right out of his still to counties all around. It is the last day of his life and he begins to wake up from his dream. He looks around him and sees that he is somewhere unfamiliar to him.

'Man, I gotta go easy on that shine, ' the man thinks as he lays down on the ground and closes his eyes and takes his last breath.

LA TUNA FISH BY MRGOODGOESHARD

10:59am January 17th, 2010

"Guilty!? Guilty!?" I hear myself ask, before everything turns into a whirling blur.

I can only compare it to the effects of the concussion caused by an IED explosion, when the ringing in your ears finally stops and the resemblance of the surrounding sounds finally returns. Its destructive power turns any faith I have left in the legal system into rubble, as I stutter out my reply to the explanation my lawyer is giving me of the judge's ruling.

"Mr. Fisher, the best thing you can do now is get your story together for prison."

"Prison! I'm going to prison!?" The seriousness in my layers of confusion doesn't trigger sympathy in my lawyer's expression. I look up at the approaching bailiff and hold on to my lawyer's thousand dollar suit as tight as I can with my cuffed hands.

Being an out of shape, middle aged, white man, I know in my heart, I won't survive long in prison, especially with the charge I've just been convicted of. I've never been racist, but as I silently plead to my black lawyer, with my eyes, to do something, he smuggly snatches his arm free.

He had represented me, and the judge has passed his judgement, so technically his job was done, but dammit I expect more. I deserve more. I glance past the judge, filled with defiance, thinking Lady Liberty might be my last shot.

"You must have really believed in White Privilege, huh? Well you know that bitch is blind right?" my lawyer points out, chuckling under his breath. "Look when you get there, just tell everyone you're in for embezzlement or something. Isn't that the type of crimes you guys always commit?"

He runs his hand down the sleeve of his sports coat to smooth out the wrinkles I caused, with a look of irritation plastered across his face as if I'd somehow soiled him. I don't remember seeing any irritation when I paid his 10 thousand dollar retainer, that's for sure.

The bottom of my stomach peels away, and its contents feel completely weightless when the bailiff grants me permission to hug my wife one last time. She presses her body against mine, not in an embrace, but to whisper in my ear.

"You promised me that you didn't do this. You promised that these allegations were false!"

"Honey, I didn't do..."

"Just shut up you bastard. My father warned me about you and obviously I should have listened," she sobbed.

I squeeze my eyes closed hoping that when I open them it would all be a bad dream, instead all I see is her retreating figure as the bailiff's vise-like grip leads me out of the courtroom.

7:12am December 12th, 2010

The uneven surface of the dusty highway causes my head to bang against the prison bus's window glass, waking me. Everytime I drift off, my mind takes me back to my conviction, and the circumstances that led to it. I've revisited the same dream frequently, awaiting transport to my new home, FCI La Tuna Federal Prison. From what I've gathered, it's a small compound right by the Mexico border, housing mostly Latino inmates from the Western region.

Looking for some comfort, I spin the handcuffs around my wrists and ankles to relieve the metal bite digging into my skin. The cuffs are connected to a chain around my waist, but looking out the window that caused the growing knot on my head, I don't see the point. We are surrounded by miles and miles of desert.

Two transport officers, one driving and one riding shotgun, haven't spoken a single word of English the whole trip, leaving me to feel isolated with just my own thoughts, and another agonizing moment to drift off.

11:51pm February 11th, 2008

"Is this seat taken?" she asked in a sultry, exotic, but professional voice.

By professional, I mean in a way that automatically lets me know she was a working girl. Out of town and frankly lonely, I could not think of a reason to turn down her offer.

She looked young, maybe too young, but the pancake make-up that was two shades too dark for her pale skin, made her age indefinable. I shook my head "No" as an invitation, and watched her creamy thighs spread across the red leather padded bar stool.

"So, you can look, but can't speak?" she questioned, giving me an excuse to look up into her sand colored eyes.

I take a deep breath, steeling my nerves before responding, "Nah, I mean... yeah, I can speak. I'm just a little..." I shrug, at a loss for words, then decide to just be upfront. "Honestly I've never done this before."

She laughs as if I'm the most charming man in the world. With a hand on my cheek and one sliding down into my lap, she seals the deal, "You're too cute, but don't worry I'll take good care of you, Daddy."

9:24am December 12th, 2010

I snap out of my day dream in time to eye an approaching highway sign. Anthony, New Mexico 10 miles. My apprehension kicks in thinking of all the advice, the prison stories, and the outright lies I've heard about Federal prison from the inmates at the hold-over.

What frightened me the most was the treatment of what they called, "SO's". Still lost in deep thought, I decide that I'll never label myself a Sex Offender. Never!

3:09pm April 10th, 2008

The piles of proposals that litter my desk have to atleast be looked at before I leave the office for the night. We desperately need to make a positive gain in profit before the end of the quarter or my seat will be even hotter.

Marrying the owner's daughter only gives you so much lee-way when your job is to make the company money, and you haven't been doing your job well lately. I continue to search for the metaphorical needle in the haystack, until my phone rings.

"Mr. Fisher please," the digitally scrambled voice asks.

"This is him," I immediately respond, "but who is this?" I chuckle, assuming that this has to be some sort of joke.

"I am the recipient of the 50K you are about to wire."

I'm tempted to hang up but decide to play along, besides I have a few minutes to spare.

"Oh, is that right? Why on earth would I do that?"

"Because I know the prostitute you solicited on your business trip in Seattle was born in 1992." My mouth drops open.

"I don't know what you're talking about," I whisper, then sigh, thinking about how unconvincing I sound.

How the fuck did he know about Seattle, I wonder to myself but the voice answers my question as if knowing my thoughts.

"You have nothing to worry about Mr. Fisher, once I get my 50K. I'll even mail you her identification card for your memories."

"Hold on... uh..."

"Go home and get some rest. I'll call you tomorrow morning at 9am with my account and routing numbers...and Mr. Fisher, if you contact the police, I'll contact the police. Good Night."

I wait until I hear the dial tone before I slide the phone back into its cradle.

11:15am December 12th, 2010

At first glance, FCI La Tuna looks drab and militarized like an old church for mercenaries. Once I see the 10 foot fences and 3 layers of razor wire, I start to doubt this could be a low custody prison.

As expected, the intake process was tedious and an insult to any man's sense of masculinity. After I was asked to twist and tug my genitals in front of 4 male guards, allowing them to peer into my soul's back door was a given. By then I was already emotionally and mentally numb.

Next they checked me for Covid-19 with an eight inch cotton swab, and had a temperature gun aimed at my forehead. They separated me from the Mexican inmates, and was left alone in a dingy 10' x 12' holding cell with splotched white flaking paint.

As the minutes passed, I found myself staring in space drifting.

8:53am April 11th, 2008

La Tuna Fish

At 8:53 I start watching the clock expecting the 9am phone call. Sleep was difficult to find the night before as I imagined all the hard work I've done over the years being destroyed by a distorted voice that I still wasn't sure if I should believe or not.

All morning long I fought the urge to nap at my desk while reviewing the same proposals I couldn't get through yesterday before I left work.

I look up.

8:57.

The shrill ringing of the office phone catches me off guard even though I knew it was coming. I picked up the phone determined to gain control of the conversation before it got out of hand.

"You're early."

The same digitized voice responds, with no humor, "This is not a game Mr. Fisher. Do you have a pen?"

I look across my desk, "Actually Yes, I have a whole mug full of pens. What color shall I use?"

The caller pauses then releases a deep breath, "It's obvious you are not taking this seriously. Please check your email Mr. Fisher."

I slide my mouse to awaken my computer, and click on the GMail logo.

6 notifications.

The last one has the subject line: "I'M ONLY SIXTEEN" with a .jpeg attachment.

I open it and patiently wait for the picture to download.

"Oh my God," I whisper, stricken with fear. I frantically attempt to stop and delete the download as the picture comes into full focus.

It's of me, sleep on my back, nude, in the Seattle hotel bed with the prostitute laying across my chest, also nude, holding up her ID card, and a hand written sign that say, "Yup I'm only 16!"

I immediately concede, "I don't have 50 thousand dollars." The digitized laughter is like gravel scrapping my ear drums.

"Well Mr. Fisher, I guess I'll see you in 50 years."

"No wait! I'll get it...just give me some time please," I beg, fearing the worst, but the voice had already hung up.

1:56pm December 12th, 2010

I snap out of my daydream sticky and clammy, waiting for my heartbeat to slow back to normal pace. I'll never forget that day 10 long months ago. Later that night while eating dinner with my wife, I was arrested, and haven't felt any sense of normalcy since.

The banging on the wall from the cell next to mine echoes through the concrete.

"Who are you!?" asks a loud voice.

Not sure how to respond, I say nothing.

"I said, who the fuck are you!" he repeats.

I stand on the metal toilet and scream through the vent, "My name is Charles Fisher!"

"Fisher huh? What's your charge Fisher?"

I quickly think back to my lawyer's advice. "Uh...wire fraud and embezzlement!"

SLUOS TSOL BY MRGOODGOESHARD

Curry pork or curry chicken, I wonder, trying to distract myself from the panic coursing through my veins. Leaning forward in the stiff commercial grade chair, elbows on my knees with my manicured fingers steepled,

I rest my forehead against them so my thumbs can reach around and massage my temples. The constant hum of blended voices, ringing phones, and that fucking antiseptic smell wont let me forget where I'm at for one second.

The urge to sit up straight that my father drummed into my head is undeniable, but I grow nauseated thinking of the pain pressing against the back of this chair will cause.

"Mr. Rake? The doctor will see you now. Please come with me."

I muster the energy to get up as soon as our eyes meet. Going through my mental calculations, I quickly size her up.

5'4"-5'5", yeah that's perfect, I say to myself as I spy the roundness of her thighs stretching the fabric of her navy blue pencil skirt.

Two pearl buttons of her crisp white shirt were undone leaving just a hint of toasted almond cleavage. The clipboard she held protectively across her bosom halted further examination of her body, but the placement of her hands showed no wedding ring, even though that held little merit in my mind.

"Are you ready for YOUR examination," she asked.

The way the words slid across her lightly glossed lips and the slight upward curve at their ends, indicated to me she knew exactly what I was just doing to her with my eyes.

"Sure, you lead the way," I insisted.

She eyes me suspecting something more, but dutifully turns, causing her honey blonde tipped dreads to swing then cascade down to the middle of her back.

As she leads me through the corridor past the blurred faces of the other patients awaiting attention, I eventually finish my lustful longing, ending with a sigh, at the sight of the supple peach connected to two beautifully shaped legs.

"By the way, I'm Ashley," she sings over her shoulder, "Mr. Lawry's assistant. His exam room is to the right. Please take off your shirt and put on the gown laying on top of the chair."

She pauses to assure I'm paying attention. I finally found my tongue.

"Yes of course, I can do that," I respond, trying my best to look sad.

Ashley steps towards me with concern, so I decide to flirtatiously try my luck.

"But what if I need... assistance?" I say, licking my lips.

She looks at me with no humor in her eyes, then says, "If my guess is correct as to why you are here Mr. Rake, you will definitely need a lot of assistance."

Confused, I walk past her, and close the door behind myself. I sit at the end of the exam bench-chair-table, or whatever you call this mint green folding cushioned thing. You know the one I'm talking about, with the thin paper that rolls down over it.

I'm looking incredibly silly in just my jeans, sneakers, and an open back gown in the same color family as the bench. The pain is just now starting to subside after the ordeal of trying to gently take off my shirt. The fabric rubbing and snagging against...these...things.

I jump as the door opens.

"Good morning Mr. Rake, I'm Dr. Lawry. Hope I didn't make you wait too long." I shake his extended hand.

Looking him in the face, none of his features register. It's like nothing I've experienced before. He has two arms, legs, a body, and the prerequisite lab coat, but my mind is not distinguishing his facial features.

I sit there slack-jawed as he places my file on his desk, sits down, and spins the chair towards its opening with his back to me. I'm tripping, I think to myself, and for the first time actually look around the exam room.

Anatomy charts litter the white walls, a red biohazard trash can against the corner cabinet, and the glass jar with the popsicle sticks to hold down your tongue on the counter tells me I'm in the right place. Right?

I look out the huge bay window that covers one wall, and am comforted by the sun.

My mother used to always tell me, "As long as the sun shines, everything is fine."

"Ok Mr. Rake, I want to start off with a few background questions," the faceless doctor tells me.

"OK, I'm ready," I whisper, trying unsuccessfully to stay calm.

"Age?"

"40."

"Height and weight, please?"

"About 5 feet 10 or so inches, and 189 pounds," I fudge.

"Race?"

"Black."

"Sexual orientation?"

I pause, "What?"

He turns to look at me. Well, I think he's looking at me.

He asks again, "What's your sexual preference?"

"I'm straight, but what does that..."

"How many sexual partners," he interrupts gauging my reaction.

"Nevermind, we'll get to that in a second."

He stands up, walks over to me, and goes into the drawer next to this exam bench-table-wiatever-the-fuck-this-is, and grabs a pair of gloves.

"Turn around and let me see your back," he instructs while sliding the latex gloves over his wrinkled hands.

I take a deep breath and lean over as he unties the string holding the gown together. My stomach tightens as I hear him gasp in disbelief.

"There must be hundreds of them," he says in amazement.

I drop my head in shame, embarrassed I waited all these years to get my back looked at. I wince in pain as the gown's fabric rubs against my back as he reties the knot.

"Well I guess I've answered my own question about how many sexual partners you've had."

"What do you mean Doc? What the fuck is it," I ask out of breath urging the pain to fade.

Dr. Lawry walks back towards his desk and grabs one of the many books that line his shelves before answering.

"If I'm not mistaken, it's the worst case of 'sluos tsol' I've ever seen."

Watching him thumb through his book, my vision blurs when the dam holding my warm tears breaks.

"Is it deadly? This... this whatever the fuck you just said?" My fear instantly turns into anger when I hear the Doctor chuckle.

"Not normally, but again, I've never seen a case as bad as yours."

Sluos Tsol

He sits down in his chair and rolls over to me before continuing to explain, "After your back is filled, it will move over to your stomach, then invade your arms and legs..." I zone out while he's explaining, frustrated that he still hasn't mentioned its cause. "...when it completely covers your body, they will definitely kill you," he finished.

"I've never heard of this 'sluos tsol' before. Is it common," I asked.

"Yes, in fact my assistant Ashley had some years ago when she was working herself through college."

Still confused, I finally asked the million dollar question. "What's the origin? What causes them?"

He looked me in my eyes, and in a calm calculated voice said simply one word, "You!"

The HD LED light is starting to burn my back as I lay across the exam whatcha-ma-fuckin-call-it on my stomach, as the doc takes the pictures I agree to, for the file. The hyper white camera flash gives my skin a blue/green tint. Movement across my back alarms me.

"Doc is that you?"

"No Sir, it's the sluos. They are trying to hide," he answers.

"Hide?"

"Yes, they are ashamed. Ashamed to be seen in light, ashamed of exposure."

I look over my shoulder at Dr. Lawry and even though he has no face, I still sense his excitement and intrigue. He probably has taken 10 or 15 pictures by now, I imagine. He then turns the digital camera so I can see, causing me to cringe in disgust at the sight.

The small bumps I came in with, thinking it was maybe a bad case of back-ne at worst, has grown into hundreds of red pupiled sightless eyeballs, all randomly moving in different directions pulling against my sore swollen skin as if trying to escape.

"Mr. Rake, Mr. Rake?" I blink a couple of times trying to clear my head and gather my bearings. "There you are Mr. Rake, feeling better?"

It's Ashley, I suddenly remember. How could I ever forget Ashley?

"Yeah I'm good, but why is my throat so sore?" I barely croak out.

She looks at me with contempt mixed with sympathy.

"After the doctor showed you all of the sluos, you screamed bloody murder and passed out. You've lived a horrible life Mr. Rake."

I just laid there in shock, having never passed out before, wondering why this woman could possibly hand down judgement upon me when she previously had the same affliction as me.

"Fuck all that, where is the doctor?" I quip, not having the patience for her taunting.

"He went to fill your prescription and of course show everyone pictures of your back."

I tentatively ease into a sitting position trying not to cause myself any pain.

"You're famous now," she continued, "you'll be in all the Sex Ed books and all the STD prevention ads." She walked away before I could even form a question.

Ashley exited the exam room, but before closing the door stuck her head back in.

"Always remember, everytime you con, game, manipulate, or even talk a vulnerable woman into sex with empty promises then leave, you take a small piece of something special from her Mr. Rake," she paused for a second as if thinking back to her own past before continuing, "and it stays with you for a lifetime. Looks like you've become quite the collector."

She watched my expression change from confusion, to shock, then indifference as she quietly shut the door.

The sun is setting when I walk to my car, pills in hand, repeating the dosage instructions over and over in my head, trying my hardest not to forget. Seeing my 2021 BMW across the parking lot reminds me just how great my life is.

"Fuck Ashley," I mumble under my breath. The lights flash when I hit the key fob to turn off the alarm, and unlock the doors. I gently sit down to avoid the pain from the three shots in the ass the doctor just gave me, and lean the seat back to not irritate my back. "...and fuck Dr.

Lawry too!" I say through clenched teeth as I toss the pills onto the passenger seat.

"Who am I going to fuck tonight?" I wonder coasting to a stop at the red light a few block from my apartment building. "Amy with the three kids, Lisa with the dead-end job, Melissa with the abusive husband?" I get out and walk up the stairs to the entrance.

"Nice night huh, Mr. Rake?" Sam the door attendant asks, as I walk through the opened door.

I pay him no attention and continue my thoughts, "Sasha with the funny limp?" I ride the empty elevator up to the 7th floor.

My floor, and then the familiar aroma from when I left for my appointment jogs my memory as I walk past apartment 80.

"Curry pork or curry chicken?" I wonder, thinking of Wanda, my neighbor. I run through my calculations, "31, Jamaican, divorced, no kids, long hours, lonely, vulnerable...Perfect!"

I rush into my apartment almost tripping over Stizzy, my cat, in an attempt to strip and shower in a hurry.

"Curry pork or curry chicken? Doesn't matter, I know she'll taste better than both." I laugh to myself.

I turn on the shower to let the water heat up and read the instructions one more time on the pill bottle.

Conscience (1000 MG)

Take by mouth twice daily

for the removal of "sluos tsol"

I shake my head and put the bottle down on the ledge of the sink, and turn around to see the reflection of my back in the mirror.

The pill bottle's reflection caught my attention first. "lost souls" ...and then I finally understood. Damn.

Made in the USA
Middletown, DE
23 November 2022

15440808R00047